To my little Nadine,
and to her dear papa.

Pili Mandelbaum

First American Edition 1990 by Kane/Miller Book Publishers
Brooklyn, N.Y. & La Jolla, California

Originally published in Belgium under the title *Noire Comme Le Café,
Blanc Comme La Lune* by Pastel, L'Ecole Des Loisirs, Paris.

Copyright © 1989 L'Ecole Des Loisirs, Paris, France.
American text copyright © 1990 Kane/Miller Book Publishers

Printed and bound in Italy by New Interlitho S.P.A. Milan
1 2 3 4 5 6 7 8 9 10

Library of Congress Cataloging-in-Publication Data

Mandelbaum, Pili.
You be me, I'll be you.

Translation of: Noire comme le café, blanc comme la lune.
Summary: A brown-skinned daughter and her white father
experiment to see what it would be like to have the
other's skin color.
|1. Fathers and daughters—Fiction| 2. Blacks—
Fiction| I. Title.
PZ7.M31225Yo 1990 |E| 89-24484
ISBN 0-916291-27-8

YOU BE ME
I'LL BE YOU

Pili Mandelbaum

A CRANKY NELL BOOK

Kane/Miller Book Publishers

Brooklyn, New York & La Jolla, California

"What's the matter, Anna?" her father asked. "Are you feeling sad?"
"No, Daddy."

"I'm not sure you're telling me everything," said her father.
"It's . . . it's just that I don't like it when people look at me," Anna finally admitted.
"But, why?" he asked.
"Because I'm not pretty."

"Not pretty? Why, you're beautiful."

"But Daddy, I don't like the color of my face, or of my hands or of my arms. I want to be like you."

"How silly," her father said. "I would do anything not to have this pale face of mine . . . pale just like the moon! Now let's see . . ."

"If we mix a bit of this color with a little of that color . . . that's it, now we have a nice brown. Wait a minute, I have an even better idea," her father announced.

"Let's make coffee-milk!" he suggested.
"Oh yes, Daddy, with lots of milk!"

"Now where are the coffee-filters?"

"Mommy is like the coffee, isn't she?" Anna said.

"And you are like the moon . . . no, like the milk!
And me? I'm like the coffee-milk!"

"Put in a little more milk, Daddy."
"No, that's enough; now it's exactly your color."

"Why aren't you drinking, Anna?
What's the matter?"

"I want to have hair like yours, Daddy."
"You must be joking," he replied.
"My hair's as straight as a board."

"Suppose we trade heads?" her father suggested.

"There's nothing better than coffee grounds to add some color," he said as he applied the grounds to his face.

"But how are you going to color me, Daddy?
With coffee grounds too?"
"That's going to be a surprise, Anna."

"Now help me. Spread it all over, and don't forget my neck," said her father.

"That's great. And the braids you made look terrific on me."

"Now it's your turn, Anna. I'm going to use flour to color your face.
And in a moment you'll look just like a little mime."

"What do you think?" Anna's father asked her. "Do you think Mom will recognize us? Let's go meet her and see."

"May I wear your hat?" Anna asked.

"Now she's really going to think I'm you," Anna said with great delight.

"Yes, you be me!" exclaimed her father.
"And I'll be you!" shouted Anna.

"Look, is there a circus or something in town?," a young girl asked her grandfather as they passed Anna and her dad on the sidewalk.

"Mom!," yelled Anna.

"What in the world are you two up to now?" Anna's mother wanted to know.
"Here, just look after the shopping bags while I go to buy the bread."

"I don't think Mom likes our idea very much," said Anna to her father.
"Maybe we embarrassed her," said her father.

"Look at all those women having their hair curled . . . and those having the curls taken out," observed Anna as she pointed to women in a nearby beauty parlor. "No one seems happy with the hair they have," said her father . . .

". . . nor with the color of their skin," he added.

"And now, you two clowns, it's time you both took a shower,"
said Anna's mother when they all arrived back home.

"Tell me, Mom, do you know what you get when a piece of moon falls into a cup of coffee?" asked Anna.
"You get *pluff*," answered her mother.
"No," said Anna, "you get *me*!"